For Ava

Written by

Michael Rosen

MOVING

Illustrated by

Sophy Williams

PUFFIN BOOKS

No one knows what I do.
No one knows where I go.

They see me when I come in to eat.
They see me when I sit on my chair.
They have me to tickle,
I have their laps.

Other times I am nowhere and
everywhere.
And that's how it is.

That's how it was
till the boxes came.

Old things, new things
going in,
good smells, bad smells
going in.

They saw me when I came in to eat.
They saw me when I sat on my chair.
They had me to tickle,
I had their laps.

Other times
I was nowhere and everywhere.

And it became bare.
Just boxes.
And boxes.

Still I came in to eat,
but the chair was stacked.
Still they had me to tickle,
but I had no laps.

I ate.
I was licking the last.
Soon I would go nowhere and
everywhere,
but first – the hands came for a tickle
and No.
There was a twist and a push
and I was in.

I who could go nowhere and
everywhere
was in a somewhere.
Held in.

This is what teeth are for,
this is what claws are for,
and that dark somewhere was
ripped and scarred and chewed.

But I was always in there.
Held in.

Held in
and held in,
swaying and swinging,
held in,
held in,
till there was a creak
and I was out and away.

To a where?
A new corner,
a new hole,
a new board,
a new stair,

no tickles,
no laps,
all boxes
and boxes
and boxes,

and I said:
No one knows what I do.
No one knows where I go.

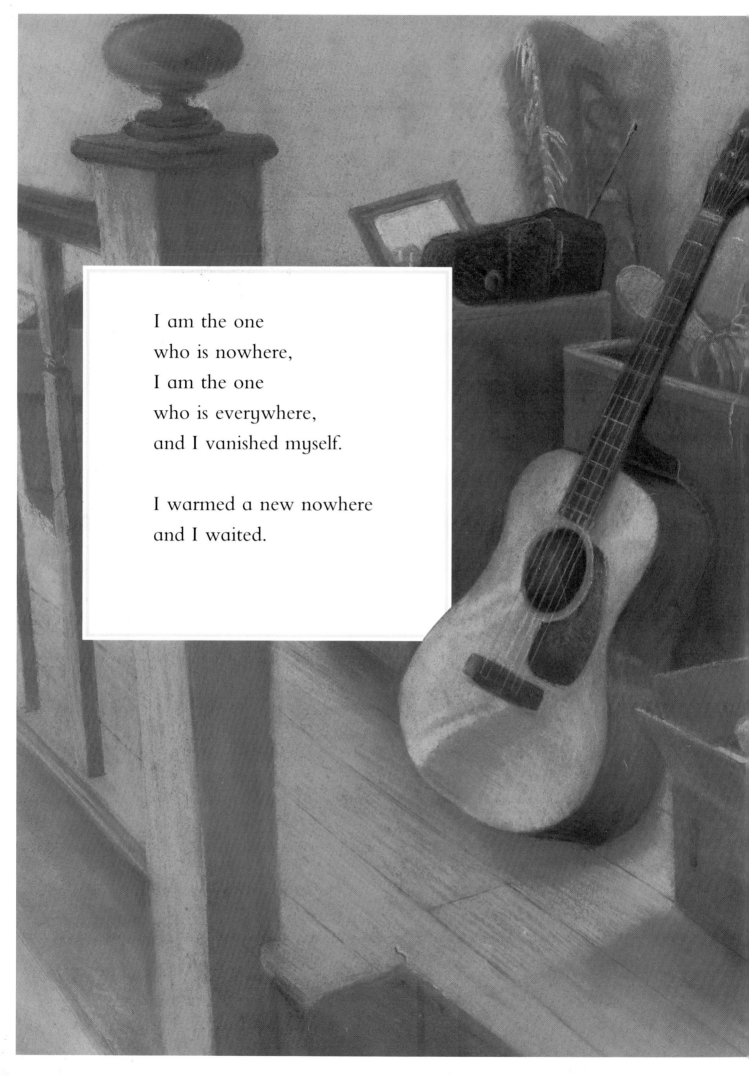

I am the one
who is nowhere,
I am the one
who is everywhere,
and I vanished myself.

I warmed a new nowhere
and I waited.

Now they will worry,
now they will be sorry,
now they will want me
to come from my nowhere,
but I won't.
Now they will want to have me to
tickle,
now they will want me to have laps,
but I won't,
I won't come
to those hands that twisted and pushed
and held me in.

You can call,
you can croon,
you can cry,
you can coo,

I won't come
into the new,
into the bare,
I won't come,

and so I sit
and grow glad
at your sadness.
For I am nowhere
and you are lost.

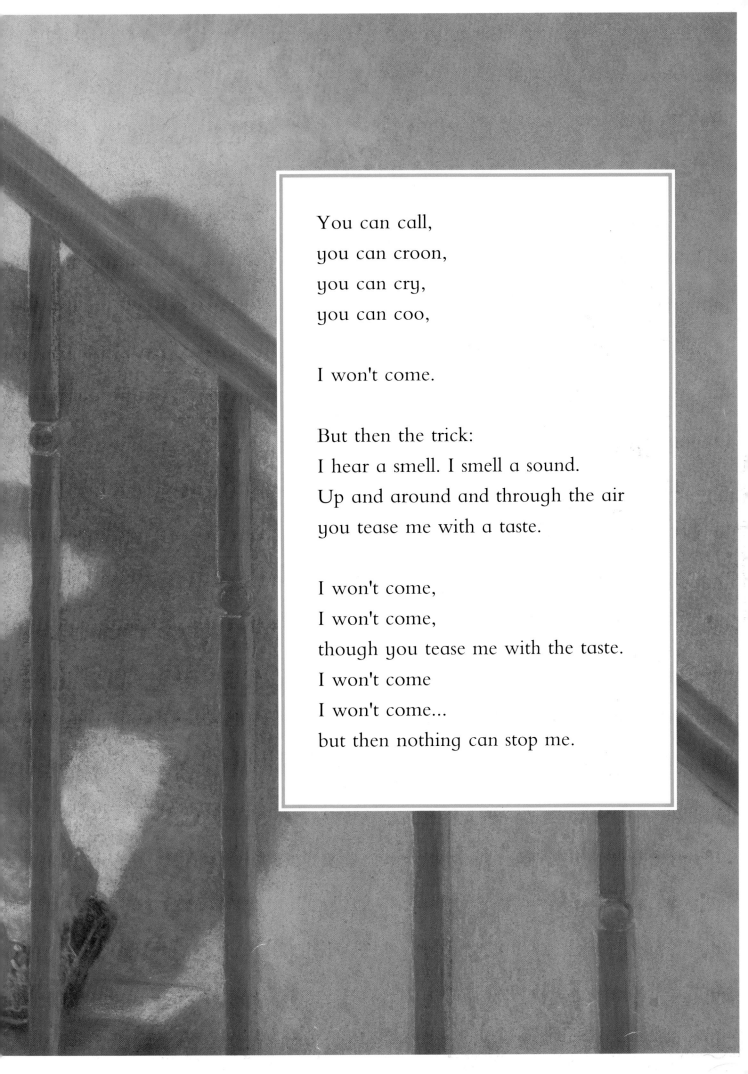

You can call,
you can croon,
you can cry,
you can coo,

I won't come.

But then the trick:
I hear a smell. I smell a sound.
Up and around and through the air
you tease me with a taste.

I won't come,
I won't come,
though you tease me with the taste.
I won't come
I won't come...
but then nothing can stop me.

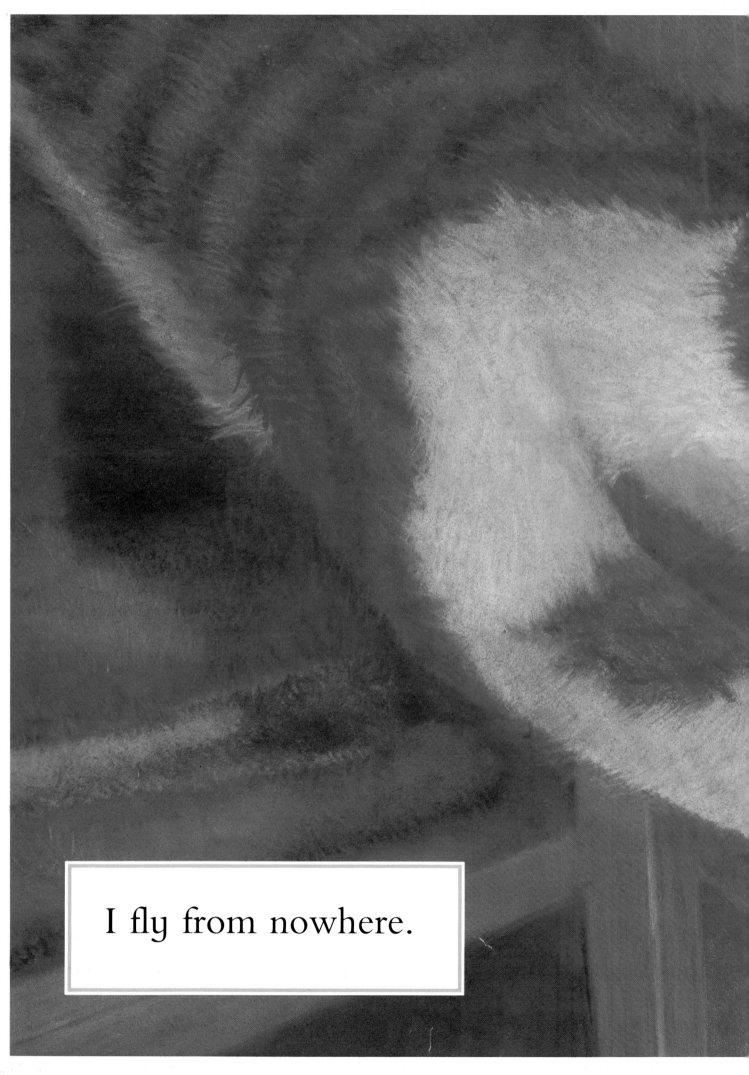

I fly from nowhere.

And they see me when I come to eat.
They see me when I sit on my chair.
They have me to tickle
and I have their laps.

Yes,
they have me to tickle,
I have their laps.

But remember this:
Other times
I will be nowhere and everywhere.

...and that's how it is.